For all the children and parents involved in
the Swansea Best Start campaign – T.D.

Farshore

First published in Great Britain 2021 by Farshore
This BookTrust edition published 2022 by Dean, part of Farshore
An imprint of HarperCollins*Publishers*
1 London Bridge Street, London SE1 9GF
www.farshore.co.uk

HarperCollins*Publishers*
1st Floor, Watermarque Building, Ringsend Road
Dublin 4, Ireland

Text and illustrations copyright © Thomas Docherty 2021
Thomas Docherty has asserted his moral rights.

ISBN 978 0 0085 8029 2
Printed in the UK by Pureprint a CarbonNeutral® company
001

A CIP catalogue record for this title is available from the British Library.

FSC
www.fsc.org

MIX
Paper from
responsible sources
FSC™ C007454

This book is produced from independently certified FSC™ paper
to ensure responsible forest management.

For more information visit: www.harpercollins.co.uk/green

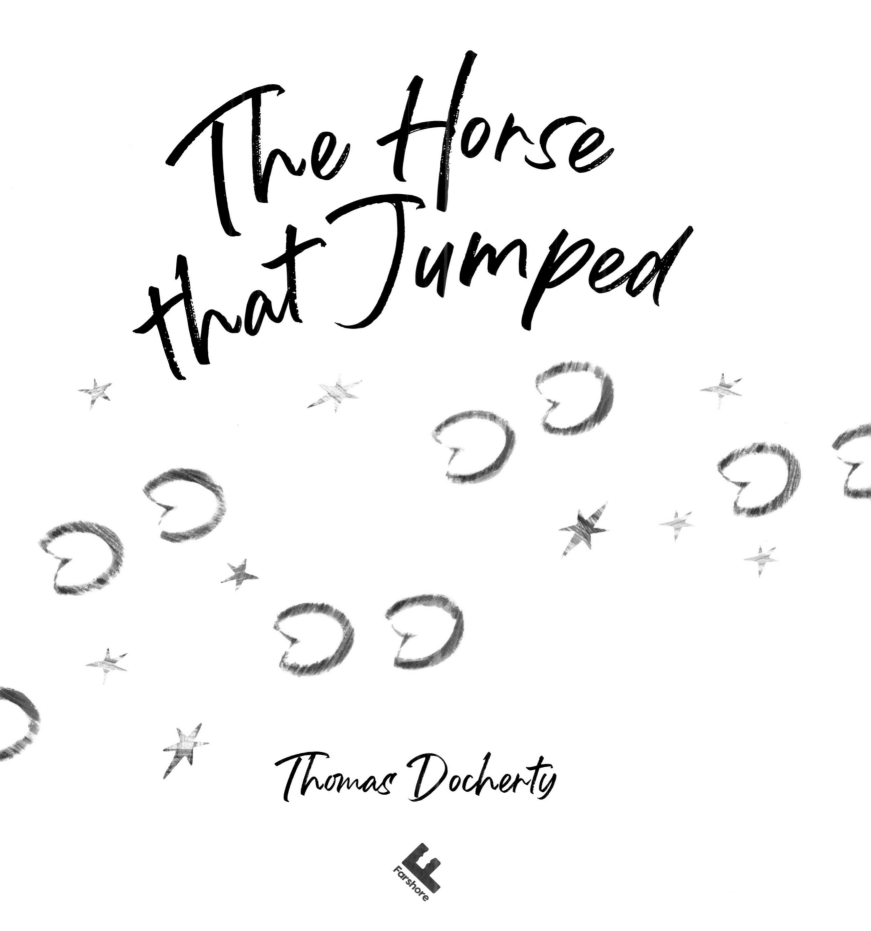

The Horse that Jumped

Thomas Docherty

Farshore

Once there was a horse that jumped

over a flower,

over a rock . . .

over a fence,
and out of its field!

It jumped across a stream, over a bench

and through
a window . . .

where it met
a girl . . .

who jumped
onto its back!

Together they galloped,

faster and faster . . .

and jumped

over the waves!

They jumped over the mountains . . .

and over the clouds.

They jumped over the setting Sun . . .

the Moon,

the stars and the planets.

Until the girl fell asleep

among the Milky Way . . .

and floated softly down

into her bed . . .

to dream.